The Incredible Water Show

Debra Frasier

Harcourt, Inc.
Orlando Austin New York
San Diego Toronto London

For those steadfast and early protectors of our nation's waters, the writers and supporters of the Clean Water Act, 1972, 1977. *How can we ever thank you?*

Whenever I have stayed on land too long, these people have helped steer me back to water: George Bunnell, Dan Frasier, Mark Hornbuckle, and Ian Hunter. Rivers of thanks.

And, as always, thanks to my editor, Allyn Johnston, for her constant belief in the strength and fluidity of the creative process, even when all signs point otherwise.

THE INCREDIBLE WATER SHOW

Written! Designed! Built! Performed!
by the
TOWER HILL PLAYERS
starring
• SAGE
• CLIFF • FOREST • RUBY
STARR • MAX
Tower Hill Festival
Free water and backstage tours
follow the show!

Library of Congress Cataloging-in-Publication Data
Frasier, Debra.
The incredible water show/Debra Frasier.
p. cm.
Summary: Elementary school students present the water cycle as acts in a play where water is the real star.
[1. Water—Fiction. 2. Hydrologic cycle—Fiction.]
I. Title.
PZ7.F8654In 2004
[E]—dc22 2003019381
ISBN 0-15-216287-9

First edition
H G F E D C B A

Manufactured in China

The illustrations in this book were made with Crayola markers and Canson papers.
The display type and text type were set in Frutiger Bold.
Color separations by Bright Arts Ltd., Hong Kong
Manufactured by South China Printing Company, Ltd., China
This book was printed on totally chlorine-free Stora Enso Matte paper.
Production supervision by Sandra Grebenar and Ginger Boyer
Designed by Debra Frasier and Linda Lockowitz

Hey! The program turned out great, Sage.
ABOUT THE TOWER HILL PLAYERS
We all worked together on a science fair project about WATER for Mrs. Page's 5TH grade at Webster School. We will earn extra credit for turning our report into this play. Please add your comments to our guest book. Enjoy the show!
The Tower Hill Players
SAGE loves anything to do with words. She got the idea for writing this story while traveling in a car, watching clouds.
FOREST is an expert skateboarder who performs at the State Fair. He wants to make movies, and he directed our show.
RUBY has studied dance since 1st grade. She also sings in the school choir. She and her mom sewed our costumes.
CLIFF plays basketball for the school team. He designed and made the dinosaur costumes and the stage curtains.
STARR is the pitcher for the All-City Champs softball team. She wrote the script with Sage and Max.
MAX likes sailing and reading about historical sea battles. He built the pirate ship and helped writ
the scrip
My picture looks stupid.
Don't forget to save one for Mrs. Page.

Welcome, one and all, to our humble stage, where we will show you positively and absolutely that you are surrounded—inside and out—by the miraculous!

Once upon a time— Yes!—once, long, long ago, a great magic occurred.
Positive hydrogen H— two tiny atoms, that is, H and H— found one negative atom, O—oxygen, that is— and together they made . . .

H₂O!
H-O-H
H2O
HOH!
And, ladies and gentlemen, upon the meeting of these three atoms, there appeared a substance of such wonder, of such power, of such beauty—

HOH!
Yes!— There appeared, suddenly or slowly, we're not sure how or why or when or where, but there it was, raining down for the first time on our planet Earth—
Yes!— Long, long ago, in the great Once-Upon-a-Time, there was . . .

GLUG, GLUG, GLUG, GLU
Now listen to this— our water is OLD! It's so old that the water you sip at supper could be the very same water that giant dinosaurs lapped up from the clear lakes of long ago.
Since its first MIRACULOUS APPEARANCE the same water has been perpetually recycling!

FANTASTIC!
Water turns into tiny, invisible droplets, and then evaporates into thin air.
ASTOUNDING!
Cool the air, and suddenly water reappears,
SQUEEZING itself right out of the sky
as mist or fog or rain or snow.
How can water do that? *Condensation,* they call it—but we call it . . .
MAGIC!

Drip. Drip. Drop, says the Water. *Solid. Solid. Solid,* answers the Rock.
Ladies and gentlemen, who will you bet on in this battle over time and space?
DROP
DRIP, DRIP, DROP!
I will tell your disbelieving ears that WATER— this gleaming trickle, this shining softness—
will drip, drip, drop a hole right through this solid rock!
But don't take my word for it. Come back in ONE THOUSAND YEARS and see for yourself—
ROCK
ROCK
the surprising, the stupendous, the strongest of them all: the Drop of Water!
STRONGEST OF ALL

SHIVER ME TIMBERS! What did I hear? "Water? What's the big deal?"
Landlubbers, have you no sense? Water IS the treasure, the X on the map, the mightiest find of all.
I've seen sights on the seven seas that would curdle your blood, but nothing is worse than a ship sailin' dry in the wind.
Aye, aye, me mates, I've been spyin' from atop me mast, and I've seen the foolish, the careless, and the greedy ice-hearted infest the cask of our fresh water with poisons and garbage—and worse!
And I've seen water plundered from its underground sources until our springs run nothin' but dirt.
SQUAWK!
WOOF!